# NEWT

An I Can Read Book®

# NEWT

Story and pictures by Matt Novak

HarperCollinsPublishers

This book is a presentation of Atlas Editions,Inc.
For information about Atlas Editions
book clubs for children write to:
**Atlas Editions, Inc.,**
4343 Equity Drive, Columbus, Ohio 43228.

Published by arrangement with HarperCollins Publishers.

1999 Edition

HarperCollins®, ♨®, and I Can Read Book®
are trademarks of HarperCollins Publishers Inc.

Library of Congress Cataloging-in-Publication Data
Novak, Matt.
  Newt / story and pictures by Matt Novak.
    p.    cm. — (An I can read book)
  Summary: In three related stories Newt, a small salamander,
befriends a mouse, defines a bug, and comforts the moon.
  ISBN 0-06-024501-8. — ISBN 0-06-024502-6 (lib. bdg.)
  [1. Newts—Fiction.  2. Salamanders—Fiction.  3. Friendship—
Fiction.]  I. Title.  II. Series.
PZ7.N867Ng 1996                                          95-13286
[E]—dc20                                                      CIP
                                                              AC

Typography by Nancy Sabato

❖

*To Jane Feder
for opening yet another door*

# CONTENTS

# FLOWER

Newt walked along the mossy bank.

Swamp slime glittered

in the bright sunlight,

and mud squished between his toes.

"What a perfect day,"

Newt said.

"I wish I could keep it for always."

Then Newt saw a beautiful flower.

"It's perfect," he said.

"I will keep it for always."

Newt dug up the flower

and carried it home.

"Now I will never forget
this perfect day," he said.

But Newt did not have a flowerpot.

He looked in the mud,

but he did not find a flowerpot.

He looked in the swamp,

but there were no flowerpots.

Newt met a mouse

carrying a nutshell

full of water.

"That would be a perfect flowerpot,"

Newt said.

"You may have it

when I am done,"

said the mouse. "Just follow me."

14

The mouse led Newt to the place
where Newt had dug up
the flower.

"My flower is gone!"
cried the mouse.

Newt looked at the hole.

He did not say anything.

The mouse emptied his nutshell

on the ground.

"I guess I will not need this

anymore," said the mouse,

and he gave Newt the nutshell.

Newt walked home slowly.

Newt planted his flower.

"It looks different," he said.

He covered one eye.

He hopped on one leg.

He even stood

on his head,

but no matter

how he looked at it,

the flower was not the same.

"Maybe it's not perfect

after all," Newt said.

19

Newt carried the flower

back to its hole.

The mouse was still there.

"You found it,"

the mouse cried.

He hugged Newt.

They planted the flower together.

"Perfect!" said the mouse.

"Now it is," said Newt.

It was a perfect day,

and Newt kept it for always.

# BUG

One morning Newt found

a strange, fuzzy bug

on his doorstep.

"I've never seen a bug

like you before," Newt said.

"I will feed you

if you are hungry.

Then you must go home."

Newt gave the bug a bowl of honey.

The bug licked up every drop,

but it did not go away.

It just looked at Newt

with its twenty sad eyes.

A bird fluttered by with a butterfly.

"My butterfly is bright

and colorful," the bird said.

"It is a beautiful bug."

The bird and butterfly flew away.

"I've always wanted

a beautiful bug," said Newt.

Newt tried painting the bug
with colorful paints.

He tried bright ribbons.

He even put big wings

on the bug,

but nothing worked.

A rabbit hopped up

with a shiny black cricket.

"My cricket plays music,"

said the rabbit.

"It is a talented bug."

The rabbit and the cricket

hopped away.

"Maybe you are talented,"

Newt said to the bug.

"Sing with me," Newt said.

"Fa-la-la."

"Roll over!" said Newt.

30

"Let's dance," he said,

wiggling and shaking around.

The bug just sat there.

A mole rode up on a big ant.

"My ant can carry me,"

said the mole.

"It is a strong bug."

The mole rode off.

Newt sat on the bug.

"Giddyup!" he cried.

Newt hitched the bug

to a wagon of rocks.

"Pull!" Newt shouted.

The bug only looked at him

with its twenty sad eyes.

34

"You are not beautiful,

talented, or strong,"

Newt said.

"What kind of bug are you?"

The bug crawled into Newt's lap.

Newt stroked the bug.

"You are a soft bug,"

said Newt.

The bug began to buzz.

"You make a nice sound,"

said Newt.

Newt held the bug close.

"I know what kind of bug

you are," Newt said.

"You are my bug,

and that is enough."

36

# MOON

It was dark,

and Newt could not sleep.

He peeked out

a slit in his curtains.

He saw the moon

hiding behind the trees.

"You look scared,"

Newt said.

The moon was quiet.

"When I am scared," said Newt,

"I think of my best friend, Mouse."

Newt opened the curtains a little

and showed the moon

a picture of his friend.

The moon peeked

out of the trees a little.

"Then," said Newt,

"if I am still afraid,

I snuggle with my bug."

He opened the curtains further

and showed the moon his bug.

The moon peeked over the trees.

Newt saw a dark shape

in the corner of his room.

"Is that what you are afraid of?"

Newt asked.

44

He opened his curtains

all the way.

"This is just my bed," Newt said.

The moon came out

from behind the trees.

"See," said Newt,

"it's not so dark after all."

They smiled at each other.

Then Newt went to sleep,

and the bright, brave moon

watched over him.